It All Began When I Said YES

Simon Philip &
Annabel Tempest

SIMON & SCHUSTER
London   New York   Sydney   Toronto   New Delhi

It all began when I said yes.
Mum and Dad were always suggesting
things that I really didn't want,
so OF COURSE I said no.

"Can you sit up straight
to eat your food?"

"No!"

"Would you like
more broccoli?"

"No way!"

"Will you brush your hair now?"

"Not a chance!"

They got fed up with me saying no.
"Why can't you just say yes for once?" they said.

I promised I would try.

So it was a little bit unlucky that it was me
who opened the door to . . .

… an excited-looking gorilla called Gideon.
He started asking questions straight away.

"Do you have a scooter by any chance?"

I said that I did.

"May I have a ride?"

He looked a bit heavy, but I didn't want to be rude.
And Mum and Dad HAD asked me to say yes more often.

I was right. Gideon was HEAVY.
Luckily, he kept wanting to stop.

He seemed to have a lot to get done.
Even for a gorilla.

First of all we stopped so Gideon
could buy a very fetching hat.

Then Gideon saw a very bright shirt in a shop window,
and decided that he absolutely had to have it,
so we stopped there as well.

It was a bit of a tight fit, and I'm not sure it was his colour, but he asked if it looked nice.

I said yes.

After stopping to buy
a bucket-load of bananas,

a tower of paper plates,
a mountain of jelly,

some very colourful
streamers

and more hats in the
shape of cones . . .

... Gideon finally came out of a shop with so many balloons I was scared he might float away.

Then he stopped.
He seemed to be worrying about something.

"Do you think we need more balloons?" he asked.
I didn't know why we needed balloons in the first place.

"Yes," I said.

Gideon had a very strange shopping list.

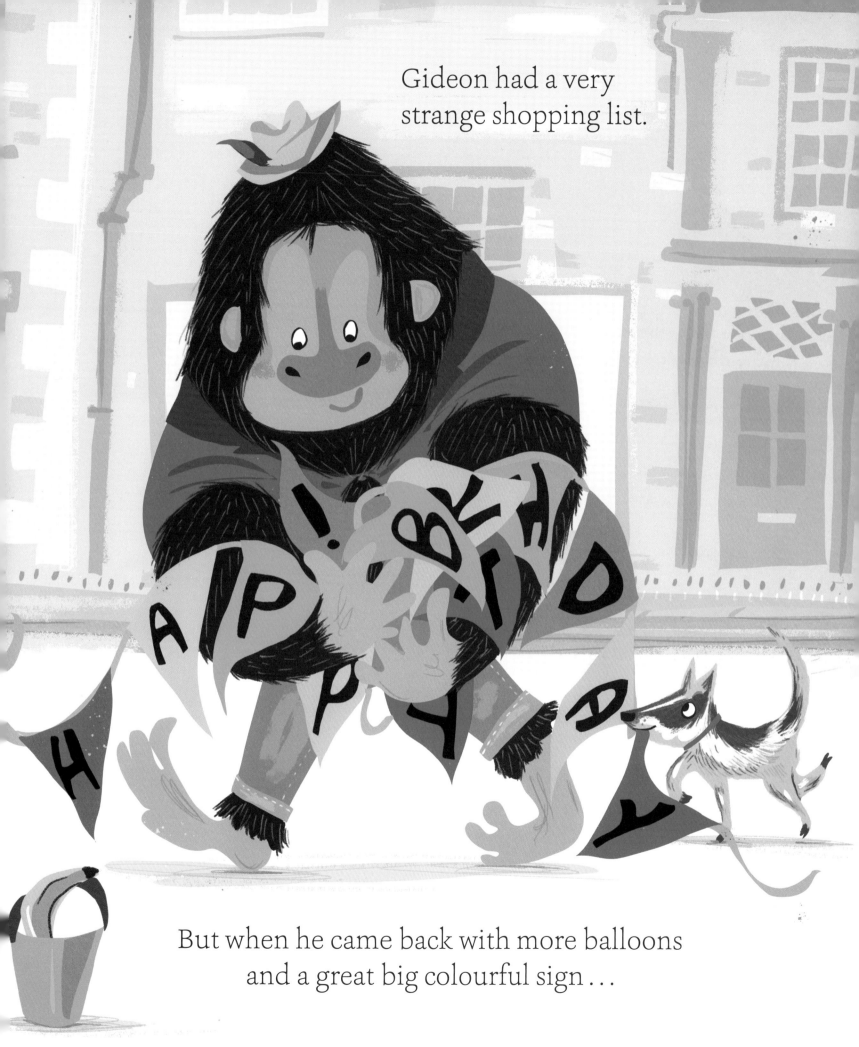

But when he came back with more balloons
and a great big colourful sign ...

… everything made sense.

"Did you know it was my birthday?" he asked.
I said yes, of course I did, and yes,
I had made him a cake.

I hoped he'd forget about it
on the journey home.

But once we were home, the questions kept on coming.
"Can we have a party?
Can we make it fancy dress?
Is there going to be a bouncy castle?"

I didn't see why not.
Gideon was already dressed
in a fancy outfit.

And the bouncy castle was still in the back garden
from Grandma's birthday party.

"Yes, yes, yes," I said.

But when the guests arrived I started to panic.

"Is this the right house?" one of them asked.
"Is Gideon here?"

Well, what could I say?!

It was all going fine until the elephants asked to play musical chairs…

the giraffe wanted to play Pin the Tail on the Donkey ...

Gideon noticed THERE WAS NO CAKE and ...

... the lion asked to eat the entertainment.

I'd never wanted to say no as much in my life!
Mum and Dad were going to be soooooo
cross with me.

But when they finally noticed all
the commotion and came downstairs,
they knew exactly what questions to ask me ...

"Do you need some help?
Shall we get rid of everyone?

Would you like a hug?"

"Yes, yes, yes!" I said.

After Mum had made a very tasty cake, everyone was happy to go home.

Especially the clown.

Dad told me that I didn't have to say yes to everything. He even asked whether I might say no every once in a while?

"Maybe," I said.

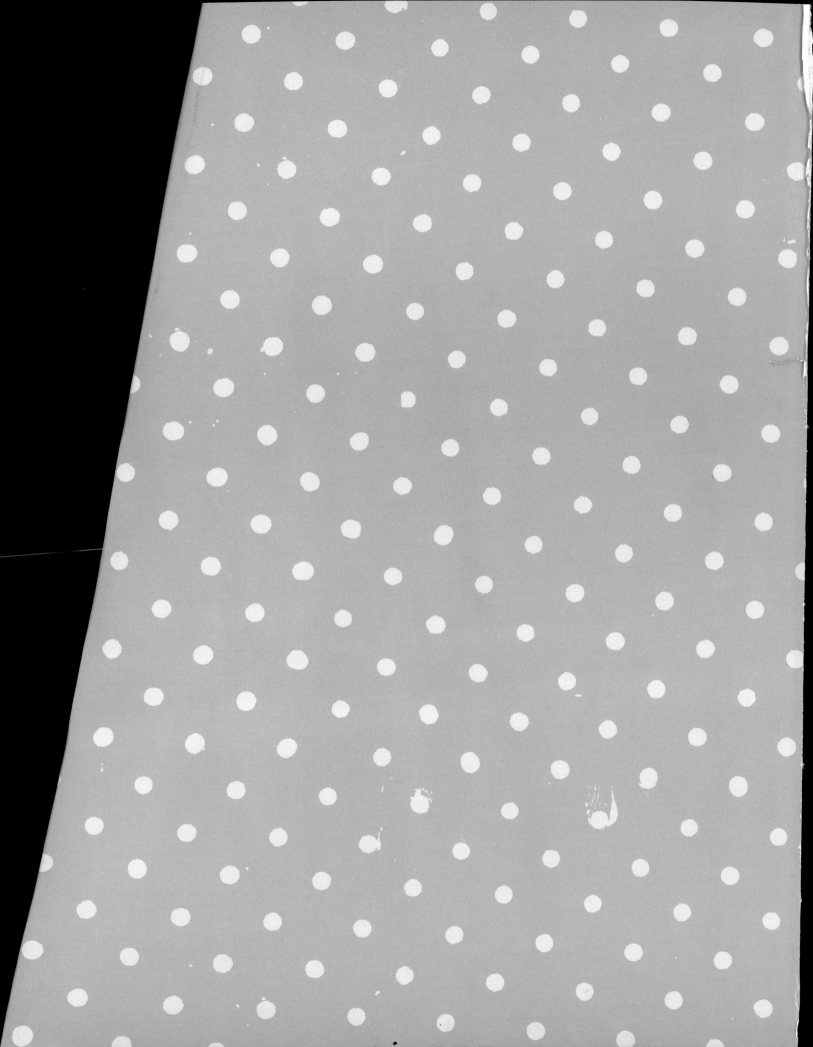

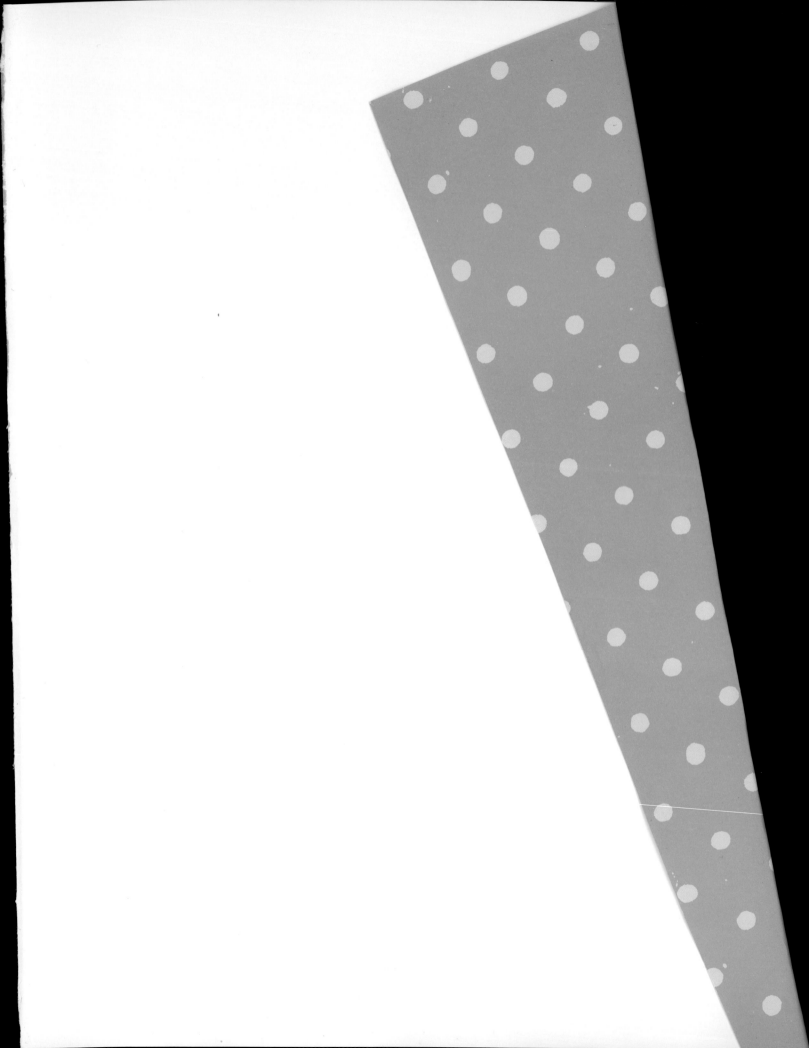